Rosemary Wood
Daniel Hall

Samurai

A Feral Kitten's Journey to Find a Home

BECKON BOOKS

Written by Rosemary Wood • Illustrated by Daniel Hole

Daniel took his daily walk
on a cool and misty morn.

He came upon a kitten
that was dirty and forlorn.

Daniel knew the kitten was feral,
as scared as he could be.
For feral cats are wild and shy—
they're afraid of us, you see.

They stay away from people,
hoping to keep out of sight.
They have no one to feed them
and must sleep outdoors at night.

Daniel watched the hungry kitten
as he searched throughout the trash.
Would he keep on eating scraps,
or might he run off in a flash?

Daniel told his wife, Rosie,
about the kitten so small and thin.
In an instant, they decided
to put food out for him.

They set two bowls upon the ground,
under a big pine tree.
They hoped the kitten would find these,
but they had to wait and see.

Sure enough, the kitten came by,
peeking 'round the gate. . . .

As hungry as could be,
he ate and ate and ate!

"We'll take care of this kitten," Daniel said,
"with food and water each day.
He might scratch or bite, so let's not touch him.
We don't want to scare him away!"

"Then," Rosie said,
"Let's name this guy.
A kitten so brave should be
'*Samurai*!'"

Oh, but another cat lived with Daniel and Rosie.
He'd lived there quite some time.

With orange fluffy fur and dark green eyes,
he was simply known as "Nine."

Nine didn't like Samurai one bit.
He was jealous and full of spite.
There was no doubt Nine wanted him out,
which led to a terrible fight!

The cats hissed and yowled, they snarled and they growled.
Like acrobats, they flew through the air.

They tumbled and fought with their teeth and their claws.
A great cloud of dust and one big scare!

Finally Nine crouched in the ivy,
just as mad as he could be.
He'd tried and he'd tried,
but Samurai just wouldn't flee.

Samurai always returned to his spot near the tree,
waiting for supper each night.
And Nine finally got used to the new little kitten.
He no longer wanted to fight.

It took a long time to earn Samurai's trust.

He grew tamer with each passing day.

Fat and content, with a shiny clean coat,

he clearly wanted to stay.

Then, Samurai walked into the house.

This came as quite a surprise.

The brave little kitten marched right through the door.

Daniel could hardly believe his eyes!

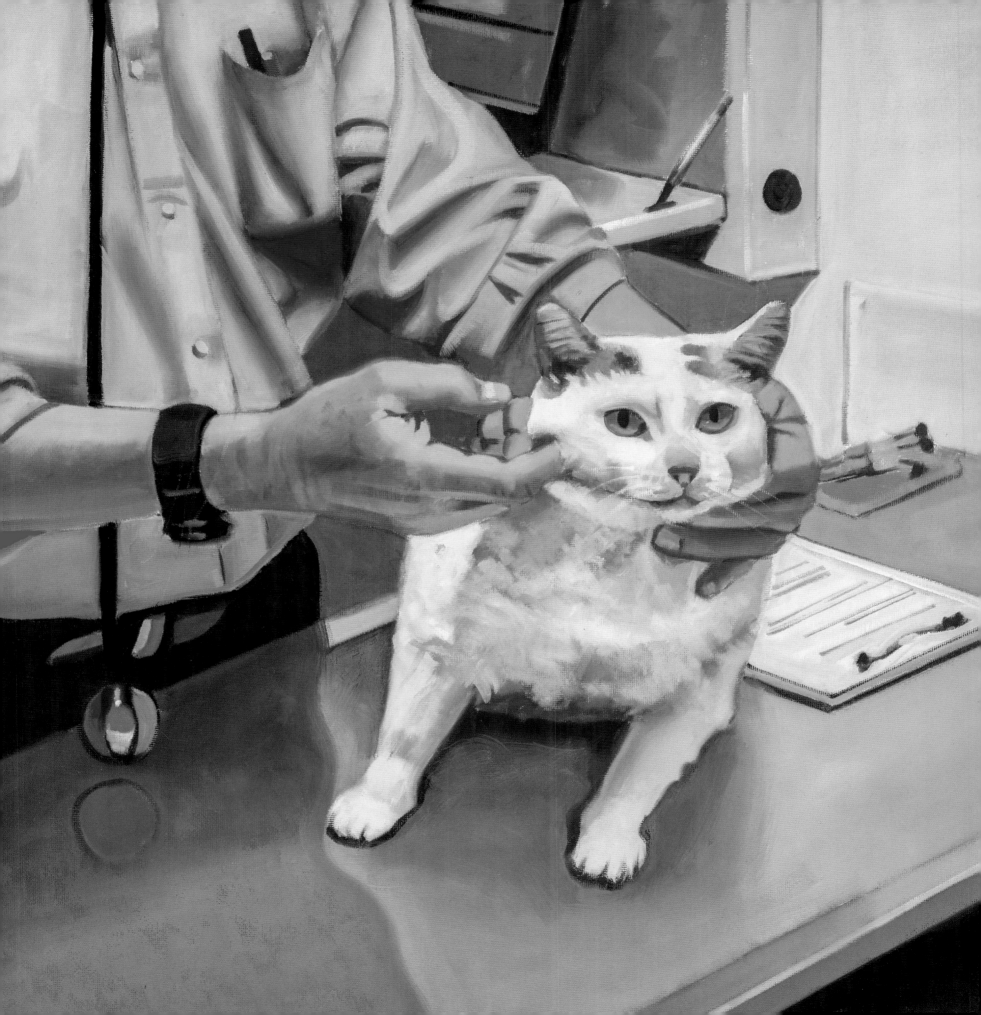

Daniel and Rosie loved Samurai.
They knew he'd make a great pet.
But he'd never had shots or a checkup,
so they took him to visit the vet.

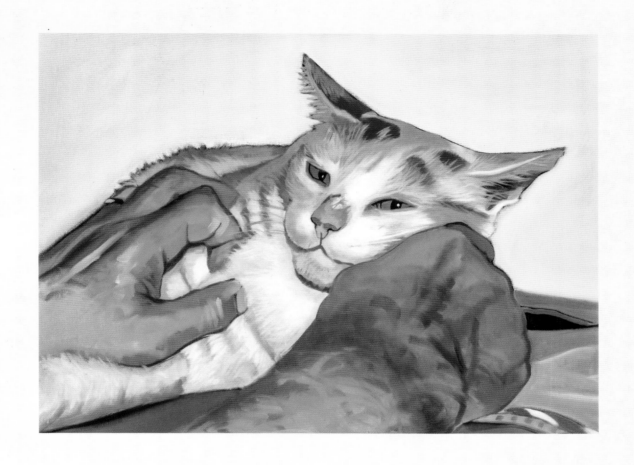

Samurai now had a home.

He always appeared in time to be fed.

Best of all, he lived his days playing outside

and his nights tucked snugly in bed.

Feral cats are domesticated cats that have returned to the wild, or the offspring of feral cats. They are different from strays, which are pets that have been lost or abandoned. The offspring of stray cats can be considered feral if born in the wild. Feral cats are not used to human contact.

There are an estimated thirty to forty million feral and stray cats in the United States. They suffer from lack of food and medical care and often become prey to larger animals. In turn, they are a major threat to wildlife, especially birds.

Many nonprofit organizations are working to address the feral cat problem through education, rescue and adoption programs, feeding programs, and most importantly, neutering and spaying services.

On behalf of feral cats, we encourage you to find an organization near you that would welcome your inquiries, time, and donations.

Please visit *www.samuraithechildrensstory.com* for updates, art gallery, kid's page, links, and contact information.

—Rosemary Wood and Daniel Hole

 BECKON BOOKS

Beckon Books is an imprint of Southwestern Publishing Group, Inc., 2451 Atrium Way, Nashville, TN 37214. Southwestern Publishing Group, Inc., is a wholly owned subsidiary of Southwestern, Inc., Nashville, Tennessee.

Christopher G. Capen: *President and Publisher*
Betsy Holt: *Development Director*
Monika Stout: *Senior Art Director*
Kristin Connelly: *Managing Editor*
Jennifer Benson: *Proofreader*

www.BeckonBooks.com
877-311-0155

ISBN: 978-1-935442-55-4
Library of Congress Control Number: 2015904693
Printed in China